MR. SNEEZE

by Roger Hargreaves

EGMONT

This is Coldland, which is a country somewhere near the North Pole.

The weather in Coldland is winter all the time. When it isn't snowing it's freezing and when it isn't freezing it's snowing, so you can imagine how cold it is.

Because it's so cold in Coldland, everybody who lives there is cold as well.

You can tell if somebody comes from Coldland because everybody there has a red nose.

And people in Coldland aren't the only ones with red noses. In Coldland you can see red-nosed dogs chasing red-nosed cats chasing red-nosed mice.

In Coldland you can even see red-nosed elephants!

And what you hear most of the time in Coldland is a noise that sounds like this.

The sound of the sneeze is very common indeed in Coldland.

Which is not very surprising, is it?

This is the story of Mr Sneeze, who lived in a small snow-covered cottage in Shivertown, the capital of Coldland.

Every morning, Mr Sneeze woke up, sneezed, got up, sneezed, got dressed, sneezed, went downstairs, sneezed, ate his breakfast, sneezed, and went to work, still sneezing.

"I don't like this sneezing all the time," he thought to himself every day, until one day he decided to leave Coldland and try to find a cure for the sneezes.

So that very same day, Mr Sneeze packed the things he'd need for his journey (mainly handkerchiefs), sneezed, locked his front door, sneezed, and set off.

He walked and sneezed and sneezed and walked his way across Coldland, and then he sneezed and walked and walked and sneezed for days and days until Coldland was far behind.

As he walked away from Coldland he noticed that there was less and less snow. And eventually, he walked so far that there was no snow at all.

And as he walked, he noticed something else. He wasn't walking and sneezing, he was walking and walking.

For the first time in his life he wasn't sneezing.

Not at all. Not a bit. Not even the tiniest tishoo.

"I wonder why I'm not sneezing?" he thought to himself.

But he must have thought his thought out loud to himself, because a voice behind him replied, "You're not sneezing because you haven't got a cold."

Mr Sneeze jumped, turned, and there behind him stood a wise old wizard.

"What's a cold?" asked Mr Sneeze.

"A cold is what you catch when you're too cold," said the wise old wizard, wisely.

"Oh," said Mr Sneeze. "But I come from a country called Coldland where everybody is too cold all the time!"

"Nonsense," snorted the wizard. "It can't be too cold ALL the time because of the sun," and he pointed to the sun, which was smiling in the sky.

"But we don't have any sun in Coldland," said Mr Sneeze.

"No sun!" exclaimed the wizard. "How extremely extraordinarily extraordinary. We'd better do something about that then, hadn't we?"

"Yes," agreed Mr Sneeze, not quite knowing what the wizard was talking about.

"How far away is this place called Coldland?" asked the wizard.

"Oh, it's miles and miles and miles away," replied Mr Sneeze.

"In which direction?" asked the wizard.

Mr Sneeze pointed.

"Shouldn't take long," said the wizard, who then waved his wand and muttered some magic words, which wouldn't be magic if we told you what they were.

Whatever those magic words were, they worked.

Before you could say "Sneeze", both the wizard and Mr Sneeze were transported to Shivertown, which you will remember is the capital of Coldland.

As usual it was snowing.

"I say, this is a cold, gloomy place," said the wizard.

"ATISHOO!" replied Mr Sneeze, who had started sneezing again.

"Coldland certainly needs some sunshine," said the wizard. "And that's going to take some rather special magic."

"Please hurry up," said Mr Sneeze, who was rapidly turning into a snowman.

"Now," said the wizard, ignoring him. "I'm going to say some magic words, and I want you to sneeze three times immediately afterwards."

The wise old wizard then held up his magic wand and muttered some more magic words, which again wouldn't be magic if we told you what they were.

"ATISHOO! ATISHOO! ATISHOO!" sneezed Mr Sneeze.

Then quite suddenly, as if by magic, which indeed it was, the sun came out from behind the big black clouds.

And it stopped snowing.

"There now," said the wizard. "That should stop the sneezing."

And then, after muttering some more magic words, and without waiting even to say goodbye, he disappeared.

Mr Sneeze just stood there in the sunshine, watching the snow begin to melt.

After that the sun shone every day, and today Coldland isn't anything like it used to be.

You can't see red-nosed dogs chasing red-nosed cats chasing red-nosed mice any more.

And these days the sound of the sneeze is a very uncommon sound indeed.

And even Mr Sneeze doesn't sneeze any more.

And that isn't the only thing different about Mr Sneeze, as he discovered himself when he looked in the mirror one morning.

Can you see what was different about Mr Sneeze?

It happened one other time too.

See if you can find the page where that was!